WALT DISNEY PRODUCTIONS

presents

Goofy
in the
Wild West

Random House  New York

One hot and dusty day Donald,
Goofy, and Mickey arrived at
Uncle Scrooge McDuck's ranch.

"Wow!" said Goofy. "Here we are
in the Wild West! Now I can be
a cowboy."

"But Goofy, the West is not wild
anymore," said Mickey.

"I am not so sure about that, Mickey,"
said Uncle Scrooge. "Cattle rustlers have
been sneaking around the valley. They
are stealing the ranchers' cows."

"Cattle rustlers!" said Donald. "We will
help you catch them, Uncle Scrooge."
Goofy ran to get a rope.
"I will lasso those thieves for you!"
Goofy said.

Goofy tried to twirl the rope.
But he did not know how.

Down he went!

Donald, Goofy, and Mickey went off to
the bunkhouse and put on western clothes.
"Hot dog!" said Uncle Scrooge. "Goofy,
you look like a real cowboy!"

"Let me at those rustlers!" said Goofy.
"Just keep those guns empty," warned
Uncle Scrooge. "I don't want you boys
to carry loaded guns."

Goofy led the way to the corral.
But he was not used to walking in
cowboy boots.

Down went Goofy, flat on his face!
"Do you still want to be a cowboy?"
laughed Donald.

At the corral Goofy said, "Gosh! I always wanted to ride a horse."

"Here," said Uncle Scrooge. "I will let you ride the gentlest horse on the ranch."

Goofy tried to climb into the saddle.
The spurs on his boots pricked the horse.
Away went the horse—and away went Goofy!

All at once the horse stopped.
She threw Goofy off her back . . .

. . . right into a cactus patch!

Donald and Mickey pulled the cactus
needles out of Goofy's pants.

"You should get rid of those spurs,
Goofy," said Uncle Scrooge.

Goofy took the spurs off his boots
and got back on the horse.

"Whew!" said Goofy. "Riding is
hard work!"

He wiped his face with his bright
red handkerchief.

A big bull saw the red cloth.
The color red made the bull angry.
He snorted and lowered his horns.

The bull charged at the red handkerchief.
He crashed right through the fence!

Away went the horse—and Goofy, too!

Goofy and the horse rode fast
and far.

The sun was setting when they
got back to the ranch.

That night Goofy, Donald, and Mickey
were sound asleep in the bunkhouse.
"YEE-OWW!" came a strange howl.
Goofy woke up suddenly.
He reached for his gun belt.

CLUNK!
One of the guns
fell on the floor.

The noise woke
Donald and Mickey.
"Goofy, what is
the matter?" asked
Donald.

"Rustlers!"
said Goofy.
He reached
for his gun.

"YEE-OWW!" came the howl again.

"Did you hear that?" whispered Goofy.

"Yes," said Mickey. "It's just a coyote howling at the moon. Go back to sleep, Goofy. And put those guns away. You know they are empty."

Goofy put his gun belt under his pillow.
"A cowboy has to keep his guns handy,"
said Goofy.

But he had a hard time falling asleep
on such a lumpy pillow!

The next day, the sheriff came to the ranch.

"The rustlers stole more cattle last night," said the sheriff. "They are hiding down in the canyon. I am taking a posse there tonight to catch them. Will you help me?"

"Yes!" said Uncle Scrooge.
"Yes!" said Donald and Mickey.
"You bet!" cried Goofy.

"Sorry, Goofy," said Uncle Scrooge. "You
will just cause more trouble. You stay here
with Cookie and guard the ranch."

"Aw, shucks!" said Goofy.
"I will miss all the fun."

Uncle Scrooge, Donald, and Mickey
rode off with the sheriff.

"Never mind, Goofy," said Cookie. "We
have our own work to do. The posse will
be hungry when they come back. We must
make a big stew."

All day long Goofy
peeled potatoes and
carrots for the stew.

Then Goofy fed and watered the horses.
At night he led them into the stable.

Goofy and Cookie waited for hours.
But their friends did not return.
So they ate their supper by themselves.
Then they played checkers until it was
time to go to bed.

That night all was quiet at the ranch.
But not for long.
Goofy heard something.
He got out of bed.

Goofy could hear men's voices outside.

"Ha, ha! We tricked them!" said one man. "While they are looking for us in the canyon, we will steal all their prize horses!"

Goofy froze.

Those men outside were the rustlers!

Suddenly Goofy felt a tap on his back.

He jumped in alarm.

"Shhh!" whispered Cookie. "It's only me. I heard the voices too."

Goofy and Cookie tiptoed out of
the bunkhouse and hid behind the barn.
They saw the rustlers heading for
Uncle Scrooge's stable.

"Come on, men," whispered the leader
of the rustlers. "I like cattle rustling,
but I LOVE horse rustling!"

Goofy saw a
ladder against
the side of
the barn.
He started to
climb it.

"I will keep
an eye on those
thieves from
the roof," he
told Cookie.

Just as Goofy
reached the top
of the ladder,
he slipped.
The ladder leaned
backward.
"Help!" cried Goofy.

The rustlers heard the noise
and ran out of the stable.

Down came Goofy and the ladder!
Goofy landed with a big splash
in a barrel of water.

But the rungs of the ladder
trapped the rustlers.
Goofy had caught the thieves!

Cookie tied the ladder
to the ground.
Now the rustlers could not
get away.
Then Cookie built a fire
for Goofy.
Goofy was soaking wet and
shaking from the cold.

At dawn the sheriff and his posse
came riding back to the ranch.

They were tired and hungry.

And they were unhappy, too.

They had not found the rustlers.

Uncle Scrooge saw the smoke
from Cookie's fire.

"What's going on here?" asked
Uncle Scrooge.

"Hi, fellows," said Goofy
when he saw his friends.
"Are these the men you
were looking for?"

"Goofy!" cried the sheriff.
"You have caught the thieves!"

"Goofy is a hero!" said the sheriff.

"Aw, it was nothing," said Goofy.

The sheriff pinned a shiny star
on Goofy's chest.

"I am making you my deputy sheriff,"
he said.

The sheriff took the rustlers
off to jail.

Donald, Mickey, and Uncle Scrooge
waved good-bye.
Goofy proudly touched his star.
"I do belong in the Wild West
after all!" he said.

A Special Offer for members of Disney's Wonderful World of Reading ... Mickey Mouse bookplates! Your child can personalize his or her books with these big (3″ by 4″) full color nameplates, available to members exclusively. Shipped 25 to the set for just $2.00, which *includes* shipping and handling! (New York and Connecticut residents must add state sales tax). To order, simply send your name and complete address — remember your zip code — to the address below. Indicate the number of sets of 25 you wish. (These exclusive bookplates make wonderful fun gifts.) Allow 3-4 weeks for delivery.